CELEBRATION!

Jane Resh Thomas

ILLUSTRATED BY Raul Colón

Hyperion Books for Children
NEW YORK

CELEBRATION!

From where Maggie sits on the front steps, she can see both ways up and down the street. Her feet jiggle, as if they won't hold still. She spots the old car when it turns the corner. It jerks like a balky horse because Granny still hasn't learned how to drive very well since Grandpa had his stroke and landed in the nursing home.

"Picnic time!" Maggie yells into the house to Mom and Pop. "Here comes Granny!"

By the time Granny pulls up at the curb, Pop and Mom and Maggie are all lined up, while Shadow the dog prances between their legs. He gives Maggie a big slurp across her cheek. Shadow loves good times as much as anybody.

"Am I the first one here?" says Granny.

"You're always the first one here, whether it's the Fourth of July or not," says Pop with his booming laugh. "You always come an hour early. We'd be disappointed if you didn't!"

He helps when Granny's hair net snags on the edge of the door. Mom hugs her and takes the plate with Granny's famous chocolate cake. Pop hoists the gallon jugs of her special lemonade with rings of lemon floating on the top, one jug on each hip. Granny hands Maggie a jar of homemade pickles. Maggie's mouth is watering, set for all of her favorite foods, even though she ate a peanut butter sandwich ten minutes ago to keep from starving to death.

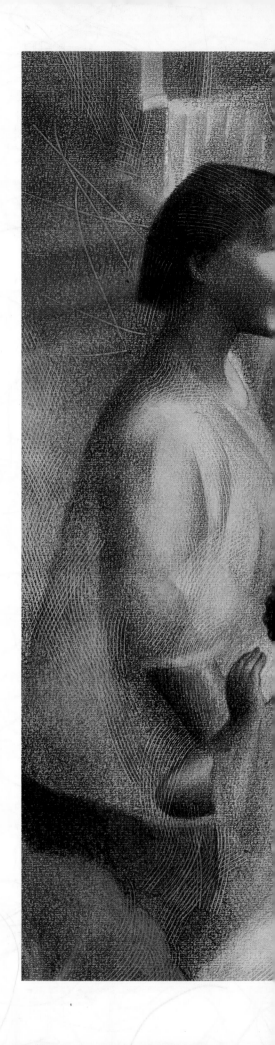

And here come Uncle Jake and Aunt Alberta in their station wagon.

"Thank goodness everybody's early," says Maggie. "I couldn't wait for the party to start." She puts her hand flat on the car window, covering the hand of her cousin Ann on the other side of the glass. Ann and Arthur and Abbie and Alice and Little Jake pile through the back doors, so excited they're practically crawling over each other.

"We brought our jump rope," says Ann.

"Carry your share of the food to the refrigerator," Aunt Alberta says, "then play." She doles out a dish of food to each of her kids. Maggie sees baked beans, macaroni salad, and pork chops under the plastic wrap.

Now Arthur and Little Jake are in the brand-new pool Mom and Dad just built. Abbie and Alice swing the rope on the back walk while Ann and Maggie jump, holding hands, alongside the picnic table Pop made out of boards laid across sawhorses. Maggie feels like Ann's sister, maybe even her twin; they jump in perfect unity.

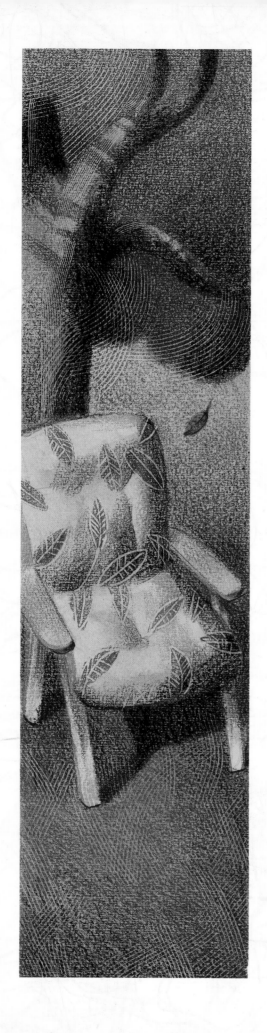

The grown-ups all sit together in the rickety lawn chairs, but Maggie notices that nobody takes the place where Grandpa used to sit, nearest the big maple tree.

"Howdy," calls Pop.

"Hi there," Mom says to the neighbors on both sides whose families have gathered for their own picnics.

Shadow climbs as far into Granny's lap as a big dog can get and licks her neck. "Some watchdog you are," she says. "If the burglars come here some dark night, you'll get 'em down and lick 'em to death."

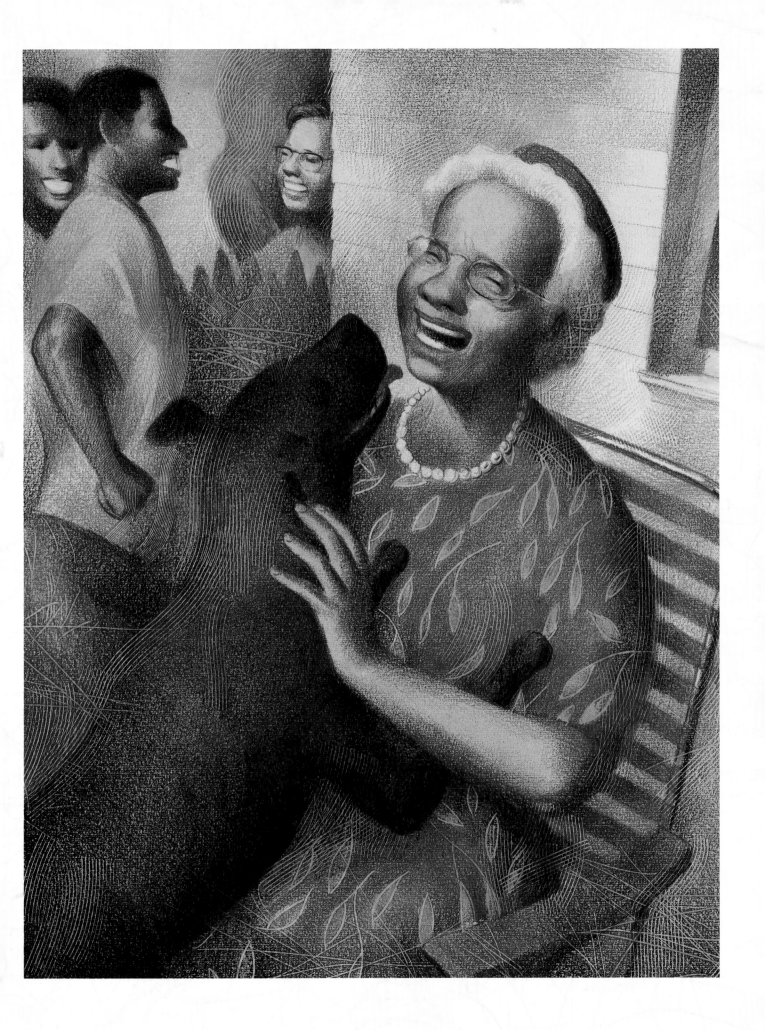

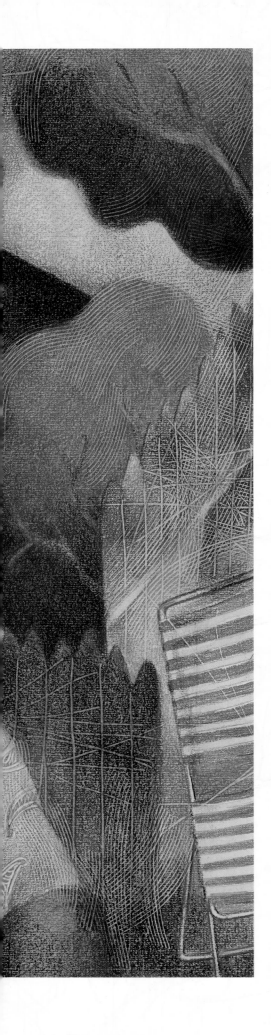

"Whoop!" says Pop. "Here's Charlie."

And up the alley, here comes that silver car Uncle Charlie and Aunt Aretha bought to celebrate when they finished law school. Uncle Charlie parks it very carefully by the garage, in the shade of the lilac bushes.

"Here comes the law!" Uncle Jake calls out. "How's everything at the courthouse?"

"Pretty good." Uncle Charlie adjusts his glasses and brushes at his Bermuda shorts. Aunt Aretha hands Mom a big bowl of raw vegetables and another one of dip.

Maurice—who wants to be called Michael, after Michael Jordan—trails along behind his folks with his face screwed up and sparks behind his eyes. At Christmas, he told Maggie he was too old for family stuff. She can see he didn't want to come. Will she be too old for Fourth of July, Maggie wonders, when she's thirteen like Maurice?

"I'm especially glad to see you, Michael," Mom says to him. "I've been warming up the basketball for a little one-on-one after the hot dogs."

Last night Maggie heard Mom whispering to Pop. "Pay special attention to Maurice tomorrow," she said. "Aretha's got him on a short leash because he pilfered some candy at the drugstore. She took him to the manager. Made him pay from his allowance and apologize."

Maggie studies her cousin's face to see whether shame shows through. She thinks of the times when she was tempted to steal. Thank goodness nobody knows; thank goodness nobody's whispering about her and some short leash! Maurice's boredom, she decides, is his way to hide every other feeling.

Uncle Charlie pokes the bottles of water he brought into the washtub filled with ice, among the cans of cola and ginger ale and the brown bottles of beer.

"Fancy bottled water, no better than out of the tap," mutters Pop, "but that's what Aretha and Charlie got to have." He sets up more lawn chairs for the newcomers, but Maurice wanders away to stand alone, leaning against the house.

Arthur and Little Jake are splashing each other in the pool, and the girls have jumped the rope a hundred and forty-eight times in a row without falling down. Now Maggie misses a beat and sprawls at Granny's feet. Shadow licks Maggie under her chin until she can't get up for giggles.

And here comes Aunt Lou, still dressed in her nurse's uniform, carrying pans of food and a beach bag and followed by her six kids.

"You look like a broody old hen," Pop calls from the barbecue, where he's trying to get the fire lit, "trailing all those chicks behind you."

Aunt Lou passes the pans off to Mom. "Vietnamese chicken wings," she says. Aunt Lou takes pride in her cooking.

"I have to test it," says Maggie. She dips her finger into the juice and licks it. "Umm," she says, ducking Lou's affectionate swat. "Aunt Lou, you're the best."

Everybody gathers around Lou as if she were a honeycomb and they were bees, all jabbering at once so nobody can hear what anybody's saying. Lou's kids burst out between the grown-ups' legs. Sally's got a Frisbee. James has brought the Hula Hoop he found in Granny's attic, from the time when Aunt Lou and Mom were girls.

A squirt gun sticks out of Leo's pocket, under his hand, where Lou can't see it. Kenny's shuffling his pack of cards; he's always practicing because he's going to be a magician and a tap dancer when he grows up. Asia has her best brown doll cradled in her arm; she's going to be a mommy. Willie's just dragging his blanket along behind him on the ground, sucking his thumb. His diapers look heavy, down around his knees.

"Best-behaved kids I ever saw," calls Pop from his place by the barbecue. "Unless it's Jake and Alberta's kids. Or Maurice. Or my own Maggie, here." He throws a wink at her.

Now Abbie and Alice and Ann and Maggie, Sally and James and Leo, and Kenny and Asia and Willie join the splashing at the pool. Maurice, alias Michael, who didn't want to come, walks up to the pool in his Chicago Bulls shirt and shorts.

"Stand aside," he says. He turns around and falls right over on his back into the water.

A wave hits Maggie in the face. "It's a tidal wave," she yells, and falls backward beside Maurice. They both come up with water streaming from their hair, giggling just like the little kids.

And here comes Uncle Frank, Mom's bachelor brother, the master of ceremonies, the bringer of fun, around the side of the house.

"Late as usual," says Granny.

"Let's put the hot dogs on the fire and give him some food before he drinks any beer," says Mom.

Maggie helps her spread bedsheets on the table and pins the corners down with rocks, in case the wind comes up. Aunt Lou's Vietnamese chicken wings are the centerpiece.

"Stick to drinking lemonade," says Granny, handing her youngest son a glass.

"Hey there, Frank," says Pop. "Have yourself a seat while I burn us some dogs!"

Maggie hugs her favorite uncle. "Did you bring 'em?" she says. "You didn't forget?"

Frank pats the long, narrow boxes in his hip pocket. "Do I ever forget?" he says. "Here's the fun, after the sun goes down. Sparklers!" He fans the boxes on the back of his hand.

"You kids dry off now." Aunt Lou tosses them the beach towels she brought in her bag and trails Mom, Granny, Alberta, and Aretha into the house. In a minute the door slams, and they all march back in a line carrying the food, as if they were delivering it on pillows to the king. They arrange the feast all up and down the table.

While Pop tends the hot dogs on the grill, Maggie snakes her hand out behind him and grabs an uncooked wiener, half for herself and half for Shadow.

"Maggie, I'm watching you with the eyes in the back of my head," says Pop. "You know we can't afford dogs for the dog."

Pop flips the hot dogs onto a plate. "Bring up your chairs, everybody," he yells, "and dig in."

O hooray for sparklers and jump ropes. Hooray for chicken wings and potato salad. O joy for Granny's lemonade, with rings of lemon floating on the top. Hooray for Uncle Frank, who cuts the chocolate cake because he's the math teacher and knows how to divide things into twenty-two equal parts.

Hooray for families who make room for everybody at picnics on the Fourth of July!

Printed in Hong Kong by South China Printing Company (1988) Ltd.

First Edition
1 3 5 7 9 10 8 6 4 2

The artwork for each picture is prepared using watercolor washes,
etched paper, and color and lithograph pencils.
This book is set in 18-point Cochin.

Designed by Ellen Friedman.

Library of Congress Cataloging-in-Publication Data
Thomas, Jane Resh.
Celebration! / Jane Resh Thomas ;
illustrated by Raul Colón. — 1st ed.
p.   cm.
Summary: Grandmother, aunts and uncles,
and assorted cousins
gather for the annual picnic in Maggie's backyard,
complete with good food and family fun.
ISBN 0-7868-0189-1 (trade) — ISBN 0-7868-2160-4 (lib. bdg.)
[1. Family life—Fiction. 2. Picnicking—Fiction. 3. Fourth of
July—Fiction.]
I. Colón, Raul, ill. II. Title.
PZ7.T36695Po   1997
[E]—dc 20   96-18421